MAX FLASH

MISSION 4

GRAVE DANGER

Go to www.maxflash.co.uk.
and enter this code:
JH3OPS11LB29
for your freebies, downloads
and other Max Flash goodies

For all staff and pupils at:
Mulberry Primary School
Osidge Primary School
Brookland Junior School
And thanks to Sonny Turner, the winner of the Max Flash Gadget
Competition with his Laser Stunner

STRIPES PUBLISHING
An imprint of Magi Publications
1 The Coda Centre, 189 Munster Road, London SW6 6AW

A paperback original
First published in Great Britain in 2008

ISBN: 978-1-84715-058-5

A CIP catalogue record for this book is available from the British Library.

Printed and bound in Belgium by Proost

2 4 6 8 10 9 7 5 3 1

MAX FLASH

MISSION 4

GRAVE DANGER

Jonny Zucker

Illustrated by
Ned Woodman

MISSION 4

CHAPTER 1

Max Flash kept his body low and crept down
the darkened corridor. His right hand was
clenched round a sleek, black Laser Bolt Gun,
and he looked around for any sign of
attackers. Suddenly, up ahead of him, a tiny
circle of light appeared.

*The Escape Dimension! I knew I was on the
right track!*

But as Max took another step, an archway to
his left flew upwards and one of the Killer
Zombies appeared, its twisted body giving off

a fuzzy silver glow. The Zombie raised a small,
brown pipe, a Death Blower, to its slimy, yellow
lips, and blew.

A steel bubble flew from the end of the
Blower and crashed towards Max, growing
larger by the second. Max raised the Laser Bolt
Gun and fired.

His aim was perfect.

Max ducked and covered his head as the
bubble exploded into a million pieces.

He quickly ran on, heading towards the light.
But within ten metres his path was suddenly
blocked as three more Zombies appeared. Max
didn't hesitate. Before they could raise their
Blowers, he fired three laser bolts in quick
succession, taking all of them down. They
collapsed to the ground one by one, and
started to melt into orangey-yellow puddles.

Gross!

Leaping over these steaming pools, Max
began to sprint again, but suddenly a large

neon-blue sign started to flash directly in front of his face.

EXERCISE INTERRUPTED! it said in huge letters.

Max cursed.

That was just getting interesting!

Reluctantly he pulled off his Virtual Battle Helmet and squinted at the bright lights of the Communications Centre that was housed under the cellar.

Max watched as the face of Zavonne appeared on the large plasma screen. As always, her hair was scraped back tightly off her face. She fixed Max with one of her trademark frosty stares.

"Hey, Zavonne," said Max.

"Hello, Max," she said briskly. "I'm sorry to interrupt your zombie-fighting practice, but something has come up that requires immediate attention."

MAX FLASH MISSION 4

CHAPTER 2

A while back, Zavonne had recruited Max as a DFEA Operative. The Department for Extraordinary Activity specialized in "unusual" goings-on – the kind of things that the official authorities knew nothing about. If it involved invisible beasts crawling through under-city pipes or slipping back into the great battles of history, it would be a case for the DFEA.

Max had been recruited partly due to his parents. Montgomery and Carly Flash were highly experienced and accomplished stage

magicians, with a flair for creating illusions, which made them the ideal DFEA recruits.

Max's parents had completed two missions for Zavonne, but in recent times it was Max that Zavonne had turned to. Growing up backstage while his parents performed their shows, he had picked up all sorts of tricks and illusions. But Max possessed another vital skill – he'd been born with an incredibly flexible body and this allowed him to squeeze into, or out of, the tiniest of spaces.

Putting all of his abilities together, Zavonne had decided Max was perfect for the DFEA. To date he'd completed three incredible missions that had taken him into the Virtual world, to distant galaxies and deep below the sea.

So as Max stared up at Zavonne's face on the screen, one thought came into his head.

What has Zavonne got in mind for me this time?

As usual, she wasted no time on pleasantries.

"Two weeks ago, near Giza in Egypt," she began, "and two miles east of the Denubi Pyramid, there was a ferocious sandstorm. After the storm had subsided, some locals found that several large stones had been uncovered. With a little further exploration, they realized they'd found part of a large, ancient building."

Max listened intently. Zavonne was an ice queen, but her missions were always filled with unexpected adventures and generous helpings of danger!

"The area was immediately sealed off," she continued, "and one of the world's top archaeologists, Professor Edmund Blythe, was called to the scene. After Blythe's initial exploration, he declared that the building was the legendary Palace of Golden Kings – home to the boy pharaoh Gazellion."

Max knew a bit about the ancient Egyptians. He'd actually listened in school when they

were doing them, especially the part about the whole gory process of mummification.

Disgusting yet fascinating!

"Gazellion was only your age when he was killed defending his palace from a man named Tulamen," said Zavonne. "After Gazellion's death, Tulamen became pharaoh."

Where is she heading with this one?

"As was the custom, Gazellion should have been buried with all of his gold and jewels inside the Denubi Pyramid."

"*Should* have?" asked Max.

Zavonne nodded. "When the pyramid was first excavated seventy years ago, a burial chamber was found, but there was no sign of any gold or jewels. Three sarcophagi were found inside the chamber, but none of them contained the mummy of Gazellion. All three belonged to his servants."

"But how did they know that one of them wasn't Gazellion?"

"In two of the sarcophagi were sets of basic serving utensils; in the third, a piece of papyrus swearing allegiance to Gazellion. So it was clear that they all came from the serving class."

"OK," said Max, scratching his head, "then where was Gazellion's mummy buried?"

"No one knows," responded Zavonne. "Exhaustive searches were made, but no sign of his burial chamber or his mummy were ever found. The whole place was eventually sealed back up to prevent robbers entering the tomb."

"Weird," mused Max.

"No," said Zavonne darkly. "That's not the weird part – that's only the background."

MAX FLASH
MISSION 4

CHAPTER 3

"Two days ago," said Zavonne, "during the course of their excavations, Professor Blythe's team discovered a fascinating piece of papyrus in the palace."

A grille on the wall next to Max bleeped and a sheet of paper slid out – a copy of the papyrus. It was covered with tiny black and gold hieroglyphs and pictures of mythical beasts, including a two-headed crocodile and a hippo with a collar of razor-sharp blades. Around the border were terrifying green and silver snakes.

"What do the hieroglyphs say?" asked Max.

"We don't know," replied Zavonne, "and nor do Professor Blythe and his team; in fact none of them has ever seen hieroglyphs remotely like these. I've circulated this image to several Egyptologists at the DFEA, but so far no one has been able to decipher them. However, we think we have identified the parchment."

"What do you think it is?" asked Max.

"We believe that the papyrus might be something known as the *Sorcerer's Venom*."

Cool name!

"Legend has it that this papyrus has dark and dangerous powers, including the ability to bring the dead back to life. It's said that it was passed down from pharaoh to pharaoh. No one knows who created the *Sorcerer's Venom*, and most archaeologists, Professor Blythe included, don't believe in its existence. To him it is a fascinating historical document, but it has no special powers."

"Where is it now?"

Zavonne looked at Max with her crystal-clear eyes. "Last night, a van left the dig site with the papyrus. Professor Blythe ordered for it to be transferred to a museum in Cairo, where a number of specialists would get a chance to study it in great detail."

Max nodded.

"But the van never got there. It was discovered in the early hours of this morning, fifty metres away from the Denubi Pyramid, completely burnt out. The driver was found in a state of severe shock. He was quivering and spluttering something about being attacked by the 'Serpents of Death'. There was no sign of the papyrus."

Max looked down at the piece of paper in his hand and stared at the evil-looking snakes trailing round its border.

"The Egyptian police say the papyrus must have been stolen by art thieves," stated Zavonne, "but I fear far darker forces are at work. If this parchment is the *Sorcerer's Venom*, as we fear, and it gets into the wrong hands, who knows what might happen."

Max swallowed nervously.

"Two of my Operatives are leaving later today for the dig site," said Zavonne. "They're called Mike Cullen and Sarah Dodd. Both of them are first-class Egyptologists, so they'll be extremely useful to Professor Blythe. However, the Professor is very strict about those who

work with him on archaeological digs. He insists that his whole team be totally dedicated to the dig 24/7, and does not permit anyone to leave the site. As a result, Cullen and Dodd's movements will be restricted. And that's where you come in."

"Er ... I know a bit about ancient Egypt," said Max, "but I'm not what you'd call a fully-loaded Egyptologist."

Zavonne ignored this and continued. "Your cover story is that Cullen and Dodd are your parents. Their childcare arrangements fell through at the last minute, so they have no choice but to bring you along on the dig."

"And this Professor guy is cool about that?" asked Max.

Zavonne frowned. "Professor Blythe did not warm to the idea. In fact, he put up quite a fight, but we pulled some strings with the people who are funding his dig and he had no choice in the matter."

Great! Zavonne's sending me out to a dig site where the main man will hate my guts!

Zavonne looked at Max with her steely eyes. "As well as doing their work on the site, Cullen and Dodd will be there to provide round-the-clock backup for you," she explained. "As you won't be a member of Professor Blythe's team, you will be in a unique position. You'll be able to slip in and out of the dig to investigate the site of the theft. In addition, your contortion and escapology skills will stand you in good stead. Sites of archaeological interest often have tiny openings an adult could never get into."

Max mulled this over. On his first three missions he'd worked pretty much alone. Having fellow Operatives on board could be excellent. On the other hand, if they were as cold as Zavonne, it could be deathly.

"Your mission is to find the *Sorcerer's Venom* and retrieve it," said Zavonne with grim

determination in her voice. "Like I said, we suspect it has fallen into the wrong hands and we are extremely concerned that whoever has it intends to unleash its immense powers in the name of evil."

"And if I don't get it back?" asked Max.

"That is not an option, Max," replied Zavonne coldly. "You have one task. Find the papyrus and bring it back to me."

MAX FLASH
MISSION 4

Zavonne eyed Max seriously. "This is an exceedingly dangerous mission, Max. There will be powers at work of which we have no knowledge. If the papyrus is as deadly and magical as we think it is, then you must proceed with extreme caution, for your life will be in constant danger. In the light of all this, we have gadgets that are tailored for the potential perils involved in this mission."

Max felt a surge of excitement. *Gadget time! Bring them on!*

A red drawer on the wall slid open.

"Take out the top item," said Zavonne.

Max picked up what looked like an ordinary football trading card, with a picture of a player heading a ball. "That is a ROCK-SOLID SCANNER," Zavonne explained. "If you press the card flat against any surface – even solid rock – it will show you any object up to two metres behind that surface. It will work for five minutes."

Max turned over the trading card and examined it.

Looking through walls? Excellent!

"The second item is a FRISBEE HOVER-BOARD."

Max pulled out a fluorescent-green Frisbee about ten centimetres in diameter. "When this Frisbee is thrown into the air, it will return to you in the form of a hover-board. This board will provide you with a one minute flight at sixty miles per hour."

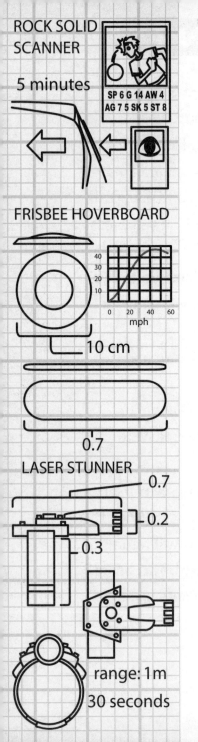

ROCK SOLID SCANNER

5 minutes

SP 6 G 14 AW 4
AG 7 5 SK 5 ST 8

FRISBEE HOVERBOARD

40
30
20
10

0 20 40 60
mph

10 cm

0.7

LASER STUNNER

0.7

0.2

0.3

range: 1 m

30 seconds

Max felt the smooth surface of the Frisbee.

Flying at sixty mph – cool!

"And the last gadget is called a LASER STUNNER," said Zavonne.

Max held up a chunky bracelet with alternate blue and gold beads.

"When you press that small button in the middle," said Zavonne, "the bracelet will fire a laser that will stun any attacker, and give you thirty seconds to escape from danger."

Max slipped on the bracelet. It fitted perfectly.

Judging by the other enemies I've faced, this could come in handy.

"Remember," Zavonne cautioned, "these gadgets should only be used to escape from immediate danger or the threat of death; they are not toys."

"Yes, Zavonne," sighed Max.

How many times do I have to listen to this lecture?

"Your plane leaves in two hours. Your father will drive you to the airport, where Cullen and Dodd will be waiting. The three of you will then catch a flight to Cairo, where a car will meet you to take you on to the dig site."

Max took in all of these details.

"And Max," said Zavonne, "this is not a holiday. I need you to find that papyrus – and fast."

But before Max could reply, the image of Zavonne had disappeared from the screen.

MISSION 4

CHAPTER 5

Max's dad drove him to the airport. He seemed pretty worried about the mission.

"It sounds rather dangerous, Max," he said.

"But I've got great gadgets, and Cullen and Dodd as backup," Max pointed out.

"True," replied his dad, "but just take extra care. Your mum and I want you to return home alive and not in some sarcophagus."

Max swallowed nervously.

What kind of deathly challenges will I be facing out there?

Cullen and Dodd were waiting in the terminal. Dad hugged Max goodbye, and wished all three of them luck. They still had an hour before their plane boarded, so they had time to grab a drink.

Sarah Dodd was an earnest woman with hazel eyes and frizzy brown hair. She looked like the kind of person who didn't laugh much.

She and Zavonne probably get on great!

Mike Cullen was more relaxed. He had cropped brown hair, and a dimple in his chin. Like Dodd, he was very focused on the mission, but it seemed to Max that he probably had a life outside of his work for the DFEA.

"We'll all keep our first names," explained Cullen, "but our surname is going to be Taylor."

Max Taylor. It sounds OK.

Dodd pulled out a map of the archaeological site. "Our living quarters are over there," she pointed out, "and the main focus of the dig is here."

Max studied the map carefully. It was weird to think that in a few hours they'd be in Egypt, looking for an ancient piece of papyrus.

"As Zavonne briefed you, Professor Blythe is very strict," said Cullen. "He likes to be in control, so Dodd and I will pretty much be at his beck and call."

"But we'll support you in whatever way we can," added Dodd, with an almost smile.

Maybe she's not quite as robotic as Zavonne!

"Obviously anything we do must be top secret," said Cullen. "As far as the Professor is concerned, the missing papyrus is just a

document of academic interest, not a nest of evil spirits and curses. We have to keep him completely in the dark about what we're doing – if he suspects for one minute that we have another agenda, he'll kick us out without hesitation."

"Understood," nodded Max.

CHAPTER 6

The flight to Cairo was half empty, so Max and his "parents" had plenty of room to stretch out. Max listened to music on his EX4 player for a while, and then slept. He woke when the plane touched down. It was early evening.

As Max stepped out on to the steps leading down from the plane, the heat hit him like a body blow. The sun was burning a golden-orange colour.

Inside the air-conditioned terminal building, the three DFEA Operatives made their way

through passport control and headed outside, where a man was waiting beside a black jeep, holding a piece of cardboard bearing the words, "TAYLOR FAMILY".

He shoved Max's rucksack and the other bags in the back, and after an hour of winding through busy Cairo streets, they left the city behind. There didn't seem to be any kind of speed limit out on the desert roads and the driver put his foot down.

It was now eight o'clock local time and darkness was falling. Cullen was sitting up front with the driver, while Max was in the back with Dodd. Up ahead he could see a faint ring of lights, and beyond them the huge, imposing shape of the Denubi Pyramid in the distance.

A few minutes later, the dig site was clearly in view. Max was amazed. It was a massive rectangular area, about the size of four football pitches. The whole place was surrounded by a high, solid-metal fence that allowed no one on the outside to look in.

"Security is necessary," the driver informed them. "The pieces they find on the dig are priceless and looters are known to try their luck."

Max thought about the stolen papyrus. *Is it the* Sorcerer's Venom*? And if so, how hard will it be to get back?*

The jeep pulled up beside a large archway. Two Egyptian soldiers cradling machine guns stood on either side of the arch. The driver handed one of them some documents.

The soldier shone his torch on the papers, and then stepped into a small sentry box. He emerged a few seconds later, holding three laminated passes on lengths of elastic, which he handed over to the driver.

"You must wear these at all times," the driver said. "Security is very tight."

The soldier then waved them on, and the jeep eased forward through the archway. They drove down a wide track and pulled up in a makeshift car park. Up ahead, Max could see a criss-cross of pathways and holes – the dig site.

The driver pointed at an area about twenty metres to their right. This section contained a large group of tents.

"Accommodation," he explained. To the left were six large marquees. "Canteen, shower block and research centres," he added, before getting out of the jeep. Max, Cullen and Dodd followed. The driver went to the back of the vehicle to pull out the luggage. They thanked him, then walked over to their "quarters".

Cullen and Dodd were given a two-person tent. Max was delighted when he was given a tent of the same size.

Excellent – a double tent to myself! Plenty of room to spread out.

He went inside, put down his rucksack and took out his sleeping bag. He then tied open the front flap of the tent and sat cross-legged in the doorway, looking out across the site.

A few minutes later, Cullen and Dodd emerged from their tent.

"Come on, Max," said Cullen, "let's get some supper."

"How's your accommodation?" asked Dodd, as they headed towards the site canteen.

"Good," replied Max, "but I'm disappointed there's no swimming pool!"

"Yeah," said Cullen, "I brought my diving gear, but somehow I don't reckon I'll get a chance to use it."

Max laughed. Dodd kind of smiled.

The canteen was situated in one of the huge marquees they'd seen when they first arrived. As they approached, they could hear the buzz of conversation.

Inside, the canteen was a hub of activity and noise. At the far end were several long serving tables, where chefs served food from large metal vats. The rest of the marquee was filled with trestle tables and benches, seating people wearing boiler suits and others in khaki uniforms.

"There's a lot of people here," observed Max, as they wove their way through the tables.

"It's huge," agreed Cullen. "But the Palace of Golden Kings is one of the greatest finds in the history of archaeology. They need a massive team. The stuff they're finding here isn't just priceless, it also tells us a great deal about how the ancient Egyptians lived."

They'd reached the serving tables and were just being asked what they'd like to eat, when a sandy-haired man with thin eyebrows and large, blue eyes came over. He had a serious expression on his face.

"That's Professor Blythe," whispered Dodd.

The Professor stopped in front of them. "Taylor and Taylor, I presume," he said, shaking hands with Cullen and Dodd.

Max reached out to shake his hand, too, but the Professor pulled his hand away and fixed Max with a withering look.

"I have never had a child on a dig before,"

said the Professor, lowering his voice, "and I
intend never to have one again."

Great to meet you, too!

"I'm sure you've heard the phrase, 'out of
sight, out of mind'," said the Professor, "and
that description will apply to you. I don't want
you anywhere near the excavations – it is not a
place for a child. Do you understand?"

"Yes," replied Max, trying not to get too angry.

"Right then," said the Professor, turning back
to Cullen and Dodd. "I'll see you both in
Examination Tent Two in ten minutes. There's
a fragment of a jug I'd like you to look at."

"We'll be there," nodded Dodd.

The Professor turned and bustled away.

"He seemed really pleased to meet me,
didn't he?" groaned Max.

"Don't worry about him," smiled Cullen.
"He's just like the things he finds on his digs –
a relic!"

CHAPTER 7

To Max's surprise the food wasn't actually that bad. He had some pitta bread and salad and a slice of apple cake to finish. During the meal, he talked with Cullen and Dodd about their mission.

They agreed that Max would visit the site of the burnt-out van tonight. It might give them some clues about who the thieves were.

"Don't spend too long over there," cautioned Dodd. "Have a quick look about, and then come back. We'll rendezvous later at the tents."

Max finished his supper, said goodbye to his "parents" and walked out of the marquee. He double-checked that his three mission gadgets were safely tucked inside his rucksack, and then headed up the path.

The guards had been told by Cullen and Dodd that Max was taking part in a school project about life in the desert, so he should be allowed to come and go as he pleased. As Max approached the two guards at the main entrance, they nodded and waved him through.

In the distance he could see the silhouette of the Denubi Pyramid. He'd calculated that he'd be able to cover the two miles there in about half an hour. The air had cooled quite a lot since his arrival, and his calculations were spot on. Within twenty-seven minutes, he was standing about a hundred metres from the base of the pyramid.

Fifty metres away sat the burnt-out Range Rover that had been transporting the papyrus.

It looked like a twisted and broken metal monster. Max walked over and shone his torch across it. The material on the seats was charred and flaking.

But who attacked the vehicle, and why was the driver reduced to such an agitated state?

Walking past the Range Rover, Max began to head towards the base of the pyramid, but he'd only gone five paces when he found himself under attack.

At first, he assumed the lines he spotted on the ground were just shadows, but then his torch picked out a series of slithery, twisting shapes that were giving off a green and silver glow.

Snakes!

He leaped backwards in horror and started to run.

MAX FLASH
MISSION 4
CHAPTER 8

The snakes were incredibly speedy, and as Max fled he could feel them lashing out at him and trying to wrap themselves around his ankles.

The Serpents of Death! The driver hadn't been hallucinating – he must have been attacked by this army of vipers! They were the papyrus thieves!

Max kicked as hard as he could, but the snakes kept striking at him – there were hundreds of them! As he ran, he reached into his rucksack and pulled out the Frisbee.

There were now two snakes curling round each shin and he could feel himself being dragged backwards. If he didn't move fast, the snakes would have him on the ground. In desperation, he threw the Frisbee into the air.

In an instant, it made a fizzing sound, crashed down to the ground in the shape of a hover-board, then flew to him.

Thank you, Zavonne!

With every ounce of strength, Max twisted and wriggled and managed to kick away the attacking snakes. He jumped on to the board and as soon as his feet made contact, it catapulted into the air.

Yessssssss!

The board accelerated swiftly as Max hurtled towards the pyramid. In the light of the full moon, he saw the snakes directly below him, their forked tongues spitting out in frenzy.

I need to lose these slithering poison shooters!

Max cruised above the pyramid, searching its stone surface for any openings. By now, the snakes were speeding up the pyramid's side, desperate for Max to fall into their path. For the first few seconds, Max saw only solid rock, but then something near the top caught his eye. It was a small circle of black – an opening – about twenty metres away. He flew straight towards it, the snakes hissing with fury below him.

He was just ten metres away when the board suddenly made a low humming sound and started to lose speed.

No! The sixty seconds must be up! I'm snake feed!

Max plummeted through the air directly towards the snakes, which were speeding up the surface of the pyramid. His feet crashed against the pyramid, followed swiftly by the rest of him. As he began to slide downwards, he threw out his hand for any possible handhold. The snakes were nearly upon him. They looked like a huge, moving oil slick, their slimy bodies twisting as they gained on their prey.

Just as he was about to fall into their clutches, Max's hand brushed against a small fragment of jutting-out rock. It was his only chance. He grabbed it and slammed to a sudden halt.

The snakes were now centimetres away. Max pulled as hard as he could on the handhold and began to clamber up the pyramid.

Up and up the crumbling side of the pyramid he went. Although he was using both feet and both hands he still kept slipping.

Where is that opening?

His hands were red raw by now, but he knew he had to keep going.

He looked round for a second. Big mistake. The snakes were faster than he was and it would only be a matter of seconds before they reached him.

But then his hand fell forward and he realized it had shot through the opening he'd seen moments before. Max swung round and squeezed his body as small as it would go, then pushed himself feet first through the hole.

He dropped about three metres before hitting the ground. Getting to his feet, he swiftly removed his rucksack and threw it up so it wedged into the opening. Above, he could still hear the hiss of the snakes.

Max breathed a huge sigh of relief. *That was close!* He wiped a line of sweat from his forehead and looked around.

He'd fallen into a narrow passageway. Behind him it bent upwards and to the left. In front of him it bent downwards and to the right.

Max pulled out his torch and started heading downwards.

He'd barely gone ten paces when he heard a noise behind him. He spun round and saw two figures on the path he'd just come down.

He froze in terror.

The figures were wrapped in tight, white bandages. They each had an amulet around their neck in the shape of a scarab beetle. One had a blue amulet, the other's was green. Through slits in the face area, he could see their dark-grey eyes staring out at him and their thin, unsmiling lips, framing hideous rows of decayed and jagged teeth.

Euuurghhh! Mummies brought back from the dead!

Max shone his torch directly in the mummies' faces to blind them for a few seconds, so he could make his escape. He started to run down the passage, but one of them called after him.

"If you diminish that cursed orb of light and state who you are, we will not attack you!"

Max slowed his pace. *Should I trust a mummy from ancient Egypt? But what choice do I have? I don't know where this passageway goes, and who knows if there are more of these creatures down there.*

Max came to a stop, turned round and shone his torch down at the floor.

OK. Time for a bit of a chat, but if those mummies try to pull a fast one, I'm back down that passage – wherever it leads.

"State who you are, intruder!" commanded the mummy with the green amulet.

"I ... I ... I'm Max," he replied hesitantly, walking towards them.

There's clearly some kind of magic at work here that's brought these mummies back from the dead. So perhaps these two know something about the Sorcerer's Venom...

"Declare the name of that mystical beam of light," said the one with the blue amulet.

"It's called a torch," Max answered.

He cut the torch's beam and the passageway fell into semi-darkness.

"Max and torch!" said the one with the blue amulet, leaning forward so that their faces were almost touching. "I've never heard such names."

Max took a couple of steps back.

This guy's breath could kill a whole army!

"I'm out here with my parents," Max explained. "We're trying to find a special piece of papyrus called the *Sorcerer's Venom*. Do you know anything about it?" he asked casually, sounding braver than he felt.

The mummies exchanged a quick glance. They stepped back a few paces and held a quick, whispered conversation.

"You haven't told me your names," said Max.

They fell silent and advanced towards him again, but Max stood his ground.

"I am Idris," stated the one with the blue amulet.

"And I am Sirus," said the other. "Your torch implement will interest the Mystical One. Return here tomorrow morning and bring it with you."

"And you'll tell me about the papyrus?" asked Max hopefully.

"Just return," said Idris.

"What about those extra-friendly serpents out there?" enquired Max. "Won't they attack me when I leave?"

"They will not bother you," said Sirus. "They only attack those who approach the pyramid. As you are leaving, they won't touch you."

"Well what about when I come back tomorrow morning?" pointed out Max. "They'll eat me for breakfast."

"The Mystical One will call them off," said Idris. "Now be gone."

Max wanted to push them further about the *Sorcerer's Venom*, but it was clear that the conversation was over.

"We will expect you tomorrow," Sirus added, before the pair disappeared down the passage.

Max thought about following them, but he was keen to get back and report his run-in with the mummies to Cullen and Dodd. So instead he headed back up the passage to his

entry point. He shone his torch over the wall.
There were some places where the stone had
crumbled away which he could use as
footholds. He listened; there were no snakes to
be heard. He clambered up, slipped on his
rucksack, then gingerly squeezed himself back
through the opening.

He looked left and right to check for his
slithering foes.

But the coast was clear – just as the
mummies had promised.

However, this didn't stop Max constantly
checking behind him as he scrambled down
the side of the pyramid; nor did it stop him
running all the way back to the site.

CHAPTER 10

Cullen and Dodd were waiting for Max in the awning of their tent, seated round a small, square table. They beckoned for him to sit down, and Cullen brewed up some cocoa on a gas stove.

"What did you find?" asked Dodd.

"Quite a lot, actually!" said Max, relieved to be back in the confines of the dig. He started with his narrow escape from the snakes, recounted his meeting with the mummies and ended with his run back to the dig site.

With each sentence he spoke, Cullen and Dodd's eyes grew larger and their faces turned whiter.

"Mummies coming back from the dead," whispered Cullen. "This is bad news."

Max pulled a piece of paper out of his pocket. It was the copy of the papyrus that Zavonne had given him. He placed it on the table in front of Cullen and Dodd. "Those snakes tonight looked exactly like the ones on the papyrus," he said. "That must be why the Range Rover driver went on about the 'Serpents of Death'. It looks like it was those snakes that attacked him, too, and stole the *Sorcerer's Venom*."

"And from what the mummies told you," mused Dodd, "it's the Mystical One – whoever he is – that's controlling the snakes; so he must have the papyrus now."

"There's one thing I don't understand," said Cullen. "If this Mystical One already has the

Sorcerer's Venom, why hasn't he used it yet for some terrifying, deadly act? Sure, he's brought those mummies back to life and unleashed the snakes, but that seems to be it... What's he waiting for?"

"Good point," nodded Dodd.

The three of them were lost in thought for a few moments.

"Well, at least I know what my job is tomorrow," said Max brightly. "I'll go to the pyramid, I'll find the papyrus and I'll steal it back before the Mystical One or anyone else can unleash its full evil powers."

Dodd bit her bottom lip. "I don't think it will be that easy," she said, "and I'm really not sure you should go back there alone. I don't like the sound of those mummies. What if they've lied to you? What if this Mystical One doesn't call off the snakes?"

Cullen took a deep breath and blew out his cheeks. "It's a risk we're going to have to take,"

he said. "Professor Blythe will know if the two of us leave the site and it could jeopardize the whole mission."

"You're right," nodded Dodd, "but I still don't like it."

She is so not like Zavonne. She has emotions!

"I'll be fine," Max said with a confident smile. But inside he felt scared. There was something about those mummies that freaked him out!

Cullen stood up. "Well, we all need a good night's sleep," he advised. "Tomorrow could be a very long day."

Max nodded and suddenly realized he was exhausted. Fighting off a giant army of snakes and meeting two mummies wasn't the most relaxing way to spend an evening.

MAX FLASH

MISSION 4

CHAPTER 11

Max woke early. He climbed out of his tent and stretched his aching limbs. His escape from the snakes last night had taken its toll. And though his sleeping bag was well padded, the sand beneath the tent wasn't quite as comfy as his bed at home. But after washing his face and brushing his teeth in the washroom, he felt a lot better.

He grabbed breakfast in the canteen with Cullen and Dodd and was just finishing when Professor Blythe collared them about some rare

chair he'd found. The Professor seemed not to notice Max at all, so he murmured a goodbye to his "parents", picked up his rucksack from his tent and slipped out of the site.

It had been warm on last night's trek to and from the Denubi Pyramid, but in the full glare of the morning sun it was baking. In fact it was so hot that Max thought he might melt. As he walked, he thought about the *Sorcerer's Venom*.

Would it be kept somewhere obvious in the pyramid or would it be fiendishly difficult to find? And who was this Mystical One?

As he approached the burnt-out vehicle, his eyes darted all around him, tense and alert in case the snakes struck again. But all was quiet and there was no sign of them. He was drenched in sweat by the time he scrambled up the side of the pyramid, and it was a relief to slip through the opening into the cool, dark interior.

There was no sign of Idris or Sirus, either, as

he dropped down into the passageway, but he could hear their voices in the distance. He flicked on his torch and followed the downwards passage. It bent right, then left, then right again.

After several more turns, he saw an opening up ahead, from which a light shone out. He switched off his torch and walked on. The mummies' voices grew louder and they were joined by a third, much deeper voice.

That must be the Mystical One!

It was hard to hear exactly what they were saying, but he did hear the word "rejoin" being used, and just before he got to the end of the passage he heard Sirus saying something about the Mystical One's powers being "diminished".

What does he mean by that?

The end of the passage opened out into a chamber with three sarcophagi to the left. It was about twice the size of his bedroom, but the ceiling was much lower.

The servants' burial chamber.

He peered in.

Idris and Sirus were standing with a third mummy. It was a head taller than the other two and had no amulet round its neck.

Max looked round the chamber, hoping to spot the *Sorcerer's Venom*, but it was nowhere to be seen.

He took a step forward.

"That's him!" declared Sirus, spotting Max.

The Mystical One stared across the chamber at Max, and then strode purposefully towards him, with Idris and Sirus at his side.

"Are you the one that possesses the magic orb?" he demanded.

Max nodded cautiously.

"I demand that you demonstrate it to me!"

Didn't they teach them any manners in ancient Egypt?

"And you are?" asked Max.

"I am Kalunga – the Mystical One – Sorcerer

to the mighty Pharaoh Gazellion!"

Max thought about what Zavonne had told him about Gazellion not being buried inside the pyramid.

"Go on, then!" snapped Kalunga impatiently. "Proceed!"

Max hesitated a second. "I will demonstrate it to you, but first I want to know if you have the *Sorcerer's Venom*?"

Nothing like coming straight out with a question!

Kalunga stared at Max with contempt. "I only have what is rightfully mine!" snapped the Mystical One. "My snakes took care of that! Now begin the demonstration."

So he does have it! If it's so secretive and deadly, why did he admit that so easily?

"Er, where are you keeping it?" Max enquired.

"ENOUGH QUESTIONS!" barked Kalunga. "I need to see the orb! If you fail to present it to me, the punishment will be BEYOND SEVERE!"

MAX FLASH MISSION 4

Max took a deep breath, flicked on the torch and swung its beam around the chamber. He held the beam on the ceiling for a few seconds, and then switched it off.

"Fascinating," murmured Kalunga, staring at the torch with interest.

"You can hold it," offered Max.

Kalunga took the torch and turned it over in his hands.

"I order you to bring me ten thousand of these orbs immediately!" declared Kalunga.

"Each and every member of my army would do well to have one."

Max looked up and down the passage, but there was no sign of anyone else, let alone a ten-thousand strong army. He stifled a snigger.

That would cost several thousand weeks' pocket money!

"That won't be possible," he replied.

Kalunga's bandaged fists clenched in rage, and he raised himself to his full height. "You laugh at me, child?" he fumed. "And you deny my request? How dare you be so insolent!"

He took a few steps forward, and Max shrank back in horror.

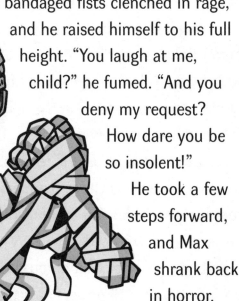

"I'm not laughing," protested Max, "and I don't have access to thousands of torches. I could probably get you three."

Kalunga's disgusting, grimy teeth ground against each other and his eyes turned a deep shade of purple. Max quickly scanned the chamber for ways out, but there only seemed to be one – the passage he'd walked down. Idris and Sirus were standing directly in front of it.

"I am growing impatient with my confinement here!" Kalunga snarled. "All I want to do is walk by the Nile during harvest time and see farmers turning shadufs in the fields."

Max swallowed nervously.

Shadufs in the fields? He remembered learning something about shadufs in school; they were some kind of farming implement the ancient Egyptians used.

Kalunga glared at Max furiously. "Oh, I may not possess my full powers at present," the

Sorcerer hissed, "but when they are restored, I WILL DEFEAT THE EVIL TULAMEN'S HEIRS! And I will congregate with my fellow members of the Sorcerer's Circle!"

The Sorcerer's Circle? Hang on a minute. Is Kalunga thinking what I think he's thinking? Does he seriously think we're still in ancient Egyptian times?

"Er ... Kalunga, can you tell me what year it is?"

"DO NOT TRY AND BE CLEVER WITH ME!" screeched Kalunga. "I am the Pharaoh's Sorcerer. I know how to make the potion! We have come back to life fifty years after the death of Gazellion."

He's made some sort of potion to bring them back to life in fifty years ... except he's got it very badly wrong.

"I hate to break this to you," Max said slowly, "but it isn't fifty years after Gazellion's death."

Idris and Sirus looked confused.

Kalunga shook with rage. "DO NOT INSULT ME!" he yelled. "I will turn you into a cockroach!"

In panic, Max quickly took off his digital watch and held it up for Kalunga to see. "Do you think they had these fifty years after

Gazellion's death?" he said. He pressed the stopwatch function, and then got the watch's alarm to beep.

"And what about the torch ... I mean orb. That was invented way after your time. You must see that!"

Kalunga gaped at all of this in stunned silence. He shook his head several times, and it was a while before he spoke again. "If what you say is true, then tell me in which time are we actually living?"

Max took a deep breath. "It's about three thousand years after Gazellion's death."

"*Three thousand years?*" Kalunga whispered in utter disbelief.

Max nodded.

Idris and Sirus gazed at each other with expressions of horror.

Kalunga's eyes narrowed in rage. "You lie!" he shrieked, snapping his fingers. Idris and Sirus immediately stood to attention. Kalunga began advancing towards Max. "Your life as a cockroach is about to commence!" screamed the mummy. "You are no match for the three of us!"

"WAIT!" cried Max in panic, imagining himself scuttling over the sand with a hard shell on his back. "I can help you!"

"HELP ME?" raged Kalunga, nearly upon Max.

"Of course!" cried Max. "You've woken up way after the end of your civilization. You know nothing about the modern world! How are you

going to achieve anything? I can bring you items from this new world that will help you with ... whatever you are planning."

Kalunga suddenly stopped.

"That idea might have merit," he said, stroking his chin. "If what you say is true, we will need items from your time. When could you bring these?"

"Whenever you want," replied Max, feeling a tiny bit less terrified. "I'm staying up at the palace."

"The palace?" said Kalunga, his eyes widening in surprise.

Max nodded. "The Palace of Golden Kings."

Kalunga gave a grotesque smile, his teeth seeming to dance in his mouth. "The Palace of Golden Kings?" He placed a bandaged arm round Max's shoulder. "Why didn't you say so before? This is truly wonderful news!"

Max shivered as Kalunga squeezed his shoulder.

"Everything is different now," said Kalunga. "We can strike a deal!"

"We can?" asked Max, flicking Kalunga's arm off his shoulder.

"Indeed," replied Kalunga. "In return for me not turning you into a cockroach, you will bring me these present-day implements and do me a small favour relating to the palace."

"What kind of favour?" asked Max suspiciously.

"I would like you to retrieve something of

great personal value," Kalunga explained,
"a family heirloom. You see that Idris and Sirus
have scarab beetle amulets round their necks?"

Max nodded.

"When I awoke I found that mine, a red one,
had been stolen. It is not worth much, but it is
of great sentimental value. It was taken from
me before I was buried down here, and I have
a pretty good idea who took it."

"Who?" asked Max.

"Inside Gazellion's palace is a workshop,"
said Kalunga. "This workshop belonged to the
Pharaoh's chief embalmer, a man named
Quodi."

An embalmer. What a delightful job!

"Quodi was – how should I put this – a bit of
a thief. He was well known for putting his
fingers into far more than dead people's
nostrils."

Gross!

"It is my belief that Quodi took my amulet

before embalming me."

Max frowned. "There is one tiny problem," he said.

"Yes?" asked Kalunga.

"The palace isn't quite how it was when you left it. It's kind of mostly buried under the sand."

"I do not want excuses!" thundered Kalunga, the sweetness suddenly gone from his voice. "Bring it back by nightfall with the modern items or you will find yourself transformed into a disgusting cockroach!"

"If I bring you your amulet, perhaps you could do me a favour in return and let me know what you've done with the *Sorcerer's Venom*?" said Max.

"I wish to hear no more words from you!" thundered Kalunga. "BE GONE!"

Max decided not to chance his luck again and headed for the doorway. But before he left the chamber, he turned round for a second.

Sirus had just handed over his beetle amulet to Kalunga, who then seemed to vanish into thin air.

Where did he go? Could it be to the place where they've hidden the Sorcerer's Venom*? I'll have to check it out when I return.*

MISSION4

CHAPTER 13

The sun was really beating down now, as Max walked back to the dig. As he pushed himself on under the scorching sun, he went over his conversation with Kalunga.

His snakes clearly snatched the Sorcerer's Venom *and he must have it somewhere in that pyramid, but where? And if he has it already, why isn't he using it? Is it because his powers are somehow "diminished"? What did the word "rejoin" refer to? And what's so special about this amulet?*

Max was exhausted by the time he arrived back at the site, but there was no time for a rest. He knew Professor Blythe had warned him to stay well away from the dig, but he had no choice. He found Cullen with another man inside a small, orange tent, examining a wooden sword.

"Dad," called Max, "can I have a word?"

Cullen looked up, then said something to the other man and walked over to Max.

"How did it go?" Cullen asked.

Max gave him a quick but detailed report.

Cullen took it all in and asked the same questions as Max about why Kalunga hadn't put the papyrus to evil use yet.

"Do you know anything about Quodi's workshop?" asked Max.

"As in Quodi the embalmer?"

Max nodded.

Cullen frowned. "The workshop's only just been dug out. Professor Blythe has ordered

that no one go in there yet, but we'll have to forget about that."

"Could you act as a decoy and get Blythe out of the way while I go and investigate?" asked Max. "I need to get my hands on that amulet – I think it might be more than just a trinket to Kalunga."

"Absolutely," replied Cullen.

Cullen quickly explained to Max where the embalmer's workshop was situated, then went off to find the Professor.

Max checked that no one was looking and rushed down the path Cullen had pointed out to him. On either side of the pathway were piles of rubble and pieces of stone jutting out from the ground at various angles. Some of these were fenced off.

A few minutes later, Max hurried down a small flight of partially uncovered stairs and found himself in the hollow shell that had once been Quodi's workshop.

Max quickly pulled the Rock Solid Scanner out of his rucksack.

OK, this can see two metres behind any surface for five minutes. I'll have to work fast, if I'm going to explore this whole room.

Max pressed the card flat against the wall to his left to activate it. As soon as he did this, he could instantly see what was behind it.

He could make out the shape of some sort of cutting implement, but no amulet. He moved the scanner up the wall, all the time seeing behind it. He carried on sweeping the card across the left wall, and then on to the wall facing him. He spied various tools and knives, but nothing remotely amulet-like.

He checked his watch and groaned with frustration. The five minutes were nearly up and there was no way that he was going to be able to scan all of the walls in here.

But then an object came into view. Max breathed a massive sigh of relief.

There it was, no more then ten centimetres behind the wall's surface – Kalunga's red amulet. And it looked like it was in perfect condition.

Max spun round. On the floor beside him was a trowel. He picked it up and immediately started vigorously chipping away at the wall. The stone started falling at Max's feet in small chunks. There were other holes in the walls so surely an extra one wouldn't draw too much attention?

Five minutes later, he could reach out and touch the front of the amulet. But its sides were still encrusted with stone.

I need to be careful here. I don't want to break it.

He dropped the trowel and picked up a small chiselling tool with a tiny metal tip. Very gently, he began to tap away at the stone, working centimetre by centimetre. Quite soon, the amulet was completely free. He reached in and pulled it out.

No sooner had he done that than the voice of Professor Blythe called out sharply, "Who is that down there?"

Max froze, amulet in hand.

Cullen must've let the Professor get away. If he finds me here it will be a complete and utter DISASTER!

MISSION 4

CHAPTER 14

Max thought about just standing there and hiding the amulet behind his back, but his cheeks were flushed and he knew he would look guilty.

He scanned the workshop in desperation. The Professor's feet were now coming down the steps.

"I said who is that?" demanded Blythe.

Max's heart raced. If Blythe found him with the amulet, he'd have to hand it over, and that meant never finding out what Kalunga was up to. Not to mention that by the end of the day he'd be a cockroach!

And then he saw a low shelf at the other side of the embalmer's workshop. A normal person would never be able to fit under this piece of jutting-out stone, but Max Flash was no normal person. He ran over and threw himself face down on the floor. He pressed himself down as hard as he could and squeezed under the shelf. He'd only just pulled in his left arm when the Professor entered.

Max forced himself as far back as possible.

"Hello?" called out Blythe.

Max listened to the Professor's impatient breathing.

Blythe started walking round the workshop. Suddenly his feet came into view. Max shrunk back. For a second, Max was convinced Blythe was going to crouch down and look straight into his hiding place.

"I could have sworn I heard someone in here," muttered the Professor. A few moments later, Max heard him going back up the steps.

Max waited a good couple of minutes before emerging, and then hurried up the steps, clutching the amulet tightly.

On reaching the top, Max checked left and right. There was no sign of the Professor or of any other member of the dig team.

Max walked quickly to the canteen. He strolled into the marquee and up to the serving counter, and took a knife from one of the cutlery trays.

He slipped it into his pocket and hurried back to his tent.

Max crawled in and zipped up the door flap behind him. He then pulled out the amulet and slid the knife under the lip of its lid. There was no give. He tried again, exerting more pressure, but still he couldn't get the lid to budge. Several beads of sweat snaked down his cheeks.

After a third unsuccessful try, he went outside and scoured the ground. A few metres away lay a small, sharp slab of rock. He picked it up and took it back into the tent.

Now it was time for brute force.

I just have to be careful not to smash it – I don't think Kalunga would be too happy about that.

Max turned the amulet on its side and brought the rock down on the join. Nothing happened.

Maybe Kalunga's put some kind of magic spell on it to stop it being opened.

But on Max's second attempt, the lid gave way and the amulet sprung open. Max took a deep breath and lifted it up.

Inside the amulet was a piece of papyrus that had been folded several times. Max's eyes widened.

What is this? It can't be the Sorcerer's Venom – *Kalunga got his snakes to grab that.*

But as Max carefully unfolded the papyrus, he instantly saw that many of the hieroglyphs were exactly the same as the ones on the printout that Zavonne had given him. And so were the pictures. There was the two-headed crocodile and the snakes round the border. Max stood there, looking in confusion at this second piece of parchment.

Is it a replica of the Sorcerer's Venom*?*

He stuffed it into his pocket and hurried off to find Cullen and Dodd. Ten minutes later they were sitting at the table in the awning of their tent, studying the papyrus.

"But I don't get it," said Dodd. "Why are there two of them?"

"Let's think this through," said Cullen. "This Kalunga guy creates a potion to make him, Idris and Sirus come back to life fifty years after Gazellion's death."

"He mentioned something about getting his own back on Tulamen's heirs," said Max, "and his ten-thousand strong army. Might his plan have been to come back to life after Tulamen was dead, reawaken Gazellion somehow and snatch back the palace?"

Dodd looked impressed. "I reckon you're spot on," she said.

Max stared down at the papyus. And that's when it suddenly hit him.

"That's it!" he whispered. "This papyrus isn't a copy of the *Sorcerer's Venom* – it must be *the other half*. Kalunga must have torn it in two to stop anyone else getting their hands on it. Quodi probably stole the amulet without

realizing what was inside. That's what the mummies were talking about! Kalunga will only get his full powers back when the two pieces are rejoined!"

Cullen and Dodd gazed at Max with open mouths. "That makes sense," nodded Cullen with admiration. "I bet his control of those snakes is limited because he doesn't yet have the whole papyrus. Perhaps his powers only work in and around the pyramid?"

"I have to take the amulet and some modern items back tonight," said Max.

"Surely we can't risk letting Kalunga get his hands on this half of the *Sorcerer's Venom*," said Dodd. "When they're rejoined, anything could kick off."

"I know," said Max. "I have to get both pieces before he does. But I have to deliver the amulet to him first. Come on, guys, I don't fancy being turned into a cockroach."

"Do you have any idea where the other

piece of the *Sorcerer's Venom* might be?" asked Cullen.

"As I left, Kalunga seemed to vanish by a wall at the far side of the chamber. I want to find out where he went."

"That could just be his magic," replied Dodd.

"It might be," nodded Max, "but it happened just after Sirus handed him his amulet."

"Definitely check it out," agreed Cullen, "but how will you buy yourself time? Kalunga is sure to open the amulet as soon as you hand it over."

"I'll trick him. I'll make him think he has both pieces, which will give me a chance to search the pyramid and find the other half. Let's seal up the amulet again, but put something in the papyrus's place," said Max.

"Hmmm," said Dodd. "But won't he be able to open it straight away?"

Cullen shook his head. "There's some amazingly powerful glue on site," he said. "If we use that, it might take him a while to crack it."

"OK," nodded Dodd, "that's what we'll do. But if you're not back in two hours, we're coming to get you, Professor Blythe or no Professor Blythe."

Max nodded, feeling the nerves fizzing up inside him like a million bubbles.

CHAPTER 15

As soon as the sky began to darken, Max made his move. Cullen and Dodd wished him serious amounts of luck, and said they'd come looking for him if he wasn't back within two hours.

As he headed to the pyramid, he went over his game plan in his head.

I give Kalunga the amulet. While he's trying to crack it open, I somehow locate the place where he vanished and try to find the other half of the Sorcerer's Venom. *I then get out of there, race back to the site and accept Cullen*

and Dodd's congratulations. Who knows, it might just work!

In his rucksack, Max carried several gadgets – exactly as Kalunga had asked. He had his EX4 player, his M-CRASH 50 games console and a mini battery-operated kettle – it was all that he could lay his hands on.

Max made good time to the pyramid. He then followed the passage down to the burial chamber, where Kalunga was waiting for him, with Idris and Sirus at his side.

"So the orb boy returns," said Kalunga darkly. "I believe you have several modern-day items for me."

Max patted his rucksack. "I have some excellent pieces of twenty-first century kit in here," he replied. "Shall I start with the EX4 player? It's hyper-cool! Check out it's record facility—"

"Let us put those aside for the moment," interrupted Kalunga. "I need to see if you have

completed your side of the bargain to escape
a future as a cockroach. Do you have my
amulet?"

He stuck out his hand expectantly.

Max reached inside his trouser pocket and
pulled out the amulet. "I've got it," he said,
showing it to Kalunga, "so you'd better keep
your promise about not turning me into a
cockroach."

"Yes, yes," snapped Kalunga, snatching the
amulet out of Max's hand. "I curse Quodi for
thievery and for delaying my plans, but now all
is ready!"

He cradled it for a second as if it was a
newborn infant, and then tried to open the lid.
It didn't budge. He frowned and tried again.

"I obviously secured it too tightly," he
muttered.

Max saw his cue and took it. Having taken
part in his parents' magic show for many
years, he had performed a variety of feats that

involved taking things off people without them noticing. The trick was to direct their attention elsewhere and to perform the grab with the utmost speed. All three of the mummies were firmly concentrating on Kalunga's amulet, so that part was taken care of.

Max darted quietly behind the mummies, and in a lightning motion snatched the amulet from round Sirus's neck. The mummy felt nothing and continued to gaze at Kalunga, whose frustration was rising by the minute.

"I WILL OPEN THIS!" he shouted angrily.

Max quickly stole over to the wall where he had seen Kalunga disappear that morning.

It's only a hunch, but it's all I've got.

He studied the surface of the wall, looking for some kind of clue. But there was nothing.

"OPEN TO ME, O AMULET!" screeched Kalunga behind him.

Max carried on scouring the wall. Suddenly he spotted something. It was very faint, but it was definitely there – an image of a scarab beetle. It was exactly the same size as the beetles on the amulets.

Max took a quick glance over his shoulder. The mummies were still struggling with the jammed lid.

Max held out the amulet and pressed it firmly against the beetle image on the wall.

If I'm right, there's something behind here. If I'm wrong...

For a few seconds nothing happened. Max could feel the sweat collecting on his forehead. He pressed the amulet harder and suddenly an opening appeared in the wall. Max didn't wait around. He jumped through the hole and heard a tiny whoosh as it sealed behind him. He found himself in a wide tunnel with a light about fifty metres up ahead.

Excellent! This must be where Kalunga vanished. But where does it lead, and will the other half of the papyrus be there?

Max hurried down the tunnel, his heart racing.

This could be the end of this mission. I could be out of here soon with the whole papyrus!

But the moment he reached the end of the tunnel he came to a halt, staring at the space that had opened up before him. It was huge – at least ten times the size of the servants' burial chamber.

Wow! Now this is something else!

Wherever you looked there was gold.

There were golden spears sunk into the ground. There were huge gold vases, and shelves housing gold plates and gold knives. And interspersed with all of this gold, there were jewels of every colour and size. Giant red rubies nestled next to turquoise diamonds.

In the exact centre of the chamber, raised on a stone platform, was a solid gold sarcophagus, with ornate silver inscriptions on its side and a blue and silver lid.

This must be Gazellion's burial chamber! No wonder no one ever found it – it can only be accessed using those amulets!

But what grabbed Max's attention more than anything else were the astonishing pictures on the chamber walls. They depicted huge numbers of Egyptian soldiers and weaponry and strange beasts – like crocodiles with two heads and hippos with collars of razor-sharp blades... They were beautifully drawn and so lifelike. And they were exactly like the pictures on the two halves of the *Sorcerer's Venom*.

Max hoped that the amulet lid would hold firm and give him enough time to find the other piece of papyrus. He looked back to the tunnel entrance. There was no sign of movement and he couldn't hear a sound.

Great! Where shall I start looking? What about Gazellion's sarcophagus?

But as he hurried over to the giant casket, two arms reached out and grabbed him.

CHAPTER 16

What on earth...?

Max twisted round. It was Kalunga and company. As Idris and Sirus held him tight, Kalunga began wrapping him in mummy bandages.

"Thought we only had one entrance, fool?" snarled Kalunga.

Max instantly thought of his Laser Stunner. He swung his arms out in an attempt to wrestle free, but he couldn't match their combined strength.

As the mummies bound him tighter still, his rucksack fell to the floor, and moments later he was completely tied up.

Kalunga shoved him to the ground beside the great, gold sarcophagus.

What is Kalunga going to do next?

"Did you really think you could get away with BETRAYING me!" screeched Kalunga. He held out his amulet. The lid was now open. Kalunga pulled out a rectangular piece of card and shoved it in Max's face.

ONE DAY TRAVELCARD, it read.

"You stole what is mine!" seethed Kalunga, "and you replaced it with this worthless piece of junk!"

Max shook his head vigorously. "It's so not worthless," he protested. "It gives you unlimited travel on buses and trains between the hours of 9.30 a.m. and 5.00 p.m."

Kalunga looked at him with contempt.

"Think about it," Max went on. "You could

catch a movie, go shopping or even visit a museum. Why not go to the British Museum? They have some of your mates in there."

"Stop this unspeakable drivel!" shrieked Kalunga, ripping the travelcard in two and throwing the pieces to the ground.

"WHERE IS IT?" he demanded. "Where is the other half of the *Sorcerer's Venom*?"

Do I lie and pretend I haven't got it, or tell the truth? I think I'll go for the truth. Kalunga doesn't appear to have the other half, so while he goes to get it, I should get a small window of time to escape from these infuriating bandages.

"It's in my right trainer," Max announced.

"What's a trainer?" asked Sirus.

"It's a shoe," Max replied.

After some partial unwrapping of bandages around Max's foot, Kalunga finally retrieved the piece of papyrus.

"MAGNIFICENT!" bellowed Kalunga, holding

the papyrus high above his head.

"We are nearing the moment for the incantation of the *Sorcerer's Venom*!" he yelled with exhilaration.

An incantation? Isn't that some kind of chant?

Max's thoughts raced. *If it is a chant, I've got an idea. But I need my EX4 player.*

Max shuffled a few centimetres towards his rucksack. He set to work on loosening the bandages, making sure the mummies weren't watching him.

The three of them were now standing looking up at a plain, clay vase that sat alone on a high wooden shelf. Kalunga waved his hand and the vase floated down towards him.

On the floor, Max was making good progress. He'd managed to work himself a little bit of space inside the bandages, and as he tugged and twisted his right arm, he could feel he was well on the way to freeing it.

Kalunga removed a piece of parchment from the vase and unfolded it.

"I WILL NOW REJOIN THE TWO PARTS OF THE SORCERER'S VENOM!" he cried.

Come on! Just a few more twists and tugs!

Kalunga slowly began to bring the halves of the papyrus together.

"REVENGE WILL BE OURS!" yelled Kalunga. Idris and Sirus stared at the parchment in awe.

Max pushed out his right arm.

I'm nearly there!

A split second later, the two pieces of papyrus came into contact with each other. Max gazed in amazement as they fused together.

I have to break free!

The index finger of Max's right hand pushed through a gap in the bandages. Then he managed to push another finger through. He stretched out for his rucksack, but he

couldn't quite reach it.

This is it! It's a do or die-a-cockroach moment!

CHAPTER 17

Max pushed out his fingers in one last effort, and to his relief he just managed to grab the top of the rucksack and inch it towards him.

"IT IS TIME FOR THE BATTLE. OUR ARMY WILL RECAPTURE THE PALACE, AND GAZELLION WILL BE PHARAOH ONCE MORE!"

Max stifled a laugh, as he unzipped the rucksack and pulled out his EX4 player.

An army? I'm sorry, but you three and some 12-year-old pharaoh kid don't constitute an army. Even if you have the Sorcerer's Venom,

*surely your four-person battle unit will be
no match for the Egyptian army, air force
and navy!*

At that instant, Kalunga began his
incantation. It was performed in a screeching,
falsetto voice.

Max was ready
for him; he
pressed down
the RECORD
button on his
EX4 player and
began to loosen
the remaining
bandages, while
keeping them
round him,
so that
Kalunga
would suspect
nothing.

Kalunga's chanting continued, but to Max's surprise nothing seemed to be happening.

Is this it? Is my punishment going to be listening to this awful sound for eternity?

Then a strange, swirling sound began to fill the chamber. To start with, it was very quiet, almost too quiet to hear. But it was getting louder by the second and the border around the papyrus glowed a dark shade of red.

Kalunga's chanting was now almost deafening, as was the great vortex of swirling noise. And then Max noticed something. At first he thought his eyes were playing some sort of fiendish trick on him.

It was the pictures on the chamber walls.

The soldiers and spear carriers and wild beasts were all starting to shake and jiggle about – a moving tableau of 2-D figures.

What on earth...?

The figures on the wall were now juddering and twitching violently.

"YESSSSSSSSSSSSSSSSSSS!" shouted Kalunga.

And then suddenly, one of the pictures – a tall, bearded soldier carrying a sleek, silver spear – turned and jumped forwards. It was a bizarre sight. A 2-D figure standing in a 3-D world.

And then slowly, the soldier's 2-D features started swelling. First his head, and then his arms. It looked like someone was using a bicycle pump to inflate him. Now his legs were pushing out and lastly his spear.

So this is the magic!

The transformation was now complete. A 2-D figure had become a 3-D figure; a real soldier; an armed soldier; a soldier who was ready for battle.

"MAY THE EXIT OPEN!" shouted Kalunga above the unbelievable din.

At the far side of the chamber, a section of the stone wall slid open, revealing a short, sandy path leading out of the pyramid.

As the soldier shook his body and adapted

to being fully-formed, a second leaped out from the wall. This guy was stockier than the first and he carried a black dagger.

"MAY OUR ARMY PREPARE ITSELF!" yelled Kalunga.

At this cue, the two soldiers straightened themselves up and marched through the opening and out into the desert.

Now a third and a fourth soldier popped out and followed their comrades outside. Then more and more soldiers started flying off the walls at a ferocious pace. As soon as they hit the ground, they made straight for the exit.

Max's eyes bulged at the sheer number of warriors.

So this is the ten-thousand strong army!

And then the beasts started coming. The first was a lion with a ring through its nose and spikes covering its entire body.

A cosy family pet? I don't think so!

Next was a line of two-headed crocodiles, with a look of blood-curdling menace on their double faces. Following on, came the hippos, with their spiky collars. Then a flock of large birds flew out, their talons as sharp as daggers.

Kalunga carried on with his chant, his eyes lit up with joy at the miraculous act he was performing.

Ten minutes later, the last of the warriors and beasts had appeared and marched outside – a massive and hideous army that would be able to take on any challenger!

A moment later, the sound in the chamber suddenly stopped and the room fell silent.

Kalunga turned his gaze upon Max, who quickly pulled his hands back inside the bandages.

"You see," said Kalunga. "My powers are immense, but only the *Sorcerer's Venom* can perform this magnificent act of reawakening!"

"Impressive," replied Max. "Now could you make these bandages 2-D and let me out of here?"

The Sorcerer ignored him and turned to Idris and Sirus. "And now it is time for us to return to our living bodies."

Kalunga pointed the papyrus at Idris and Sirus. Their bandages started unravelling at incredible speed, and Max watched as their shrivelled flesh became like new again.

In a few seconds, Idris and Sirus had resumed their human forms. They were both about twenty years old. Idris had a long, thin face and grey eyes; Sirus was plumper and had a huge shock of black hair that sat untidily on his head. They were both dressed in white servants' clothes.

"JOIN THE OTHERS!" commanded Kalunga.

Idris and Sirus hurried up the sandy path.

"And now it is my turn," hissed Kalunga, raising the papyrus above him.

His bandages started unfurling and his flesh began to fill out into a living person. He was about fifty years old, with a long, flowing grey

beard, short grey hair and small, flashing grey eyes. He was wearing a long, silver gown decorated with strange, black symbols.

"Fancy letting me out of here now?" called out Max hopefully.

"Forget it!" snapped Kalunga.

He turned to the gold sarcophagus and pointed the papyrus at it.

"Master," Kalunga whispered, "we are ready for your return." As soon as Kalunga spoke these words, the sarcophagus lid started to rise. When it was several metres in the air, it turned on its side and hovered down to the floor.

Max stared at the sarcophagus, transfixed. He felt a mix of fear and excitement as a figure began to rise from inside the casket. Very slowly, the head and chest of the figure emerged. It was the body of a boy.

It's Gazellion – right here, right now! If only I had a camera...

The boy Pharaoh was wearing an incredible blue and gold ceremonial mask, just like the one Max had seen in a programme about Tutankhamun.

Kalunga bowed low. "I will go and prepare your army, Your Highness," he said. "When you have risen, come outside to inspect your troops. Then, if all is as you wish, we will set off immediately!"

Gazellion gave him a regal nod of the head.

Kalunga looked down at Max. "As soon as our Pharaoh has inspected his army and is satisfied, I will come back to deal with YOU!" he sneered. "I will make your life as a cockroach as unpleasant as possible!"

Max swallowed in fear.

Then, with a flick of his gown, Kalunga strode out of the chamber to join the troops.

MAX FLASH
MISSION 4

CHAPTER 19

Max looked up at Gazellion, who was still sitting in his sarcophagus.

In one swift move, he threw off his bandages and got to his feet.

"Isn't that mask thing a bit hot for you?" asked Max.

The Pharaoh nodded his head, raised his hands and slowly lifted off the mask.

Sitting there was a boy who looked the same age as Max. He had smooth, tanned skin and deep-brown eyes.

"Gaz ... I mean, Your Highness," said Max, "I have been charged with welcoming you back to the world. How are you feeling?"

"Tired, but content," replied the Pharaoh, with an appreciative smile.

"It will be necessary for you to stay here for a short time," said Max, keeping one eye on the path leading outside.

"What am I required to do during this period of waiting?" asked Gazellion, with interest.

Max suddenly remembered the rest of the contents of his rucksack. He knelt down on the ground, rummaged around for a couple of seconds, then whipped out his M-CRASH 50 games console. He flicked it on.

"You are required to play Lunar Chase 2233," Max replied with a humble bow. "I will instruct you on its workings."

Gazellion pulled a confused face, but Max started to show him the controls, and then passed the console to the Pharaoh.

"What an excellent leisure-time pursuit!"
grinned Gazellion, once he'd got the hang of
the game. "I can see many happy hours on the
palace lawns with this wondrous item."

Max gave him a thumbs up. Then he
grabbed the ceremonial mask and his EX4
player and made for the exit. "I will be back
shortly, Your Highness," he said.

But Gazellion was totally engrossed in the
game and didn't look up.

MAX FLASH
MISSION 4

Outside the Denubi Pyramid stood a massive ancient Egyptian army, awaiting the boy Pharaoh. They were stationed in long rows – men and beasts. The night breeze kicked up some sand, but the massed ranks remained perfectly still. In front of them, Kalunga stood tall and magnificent, with Idris and Sirus at his side. He was still holding the rejoined papyrus in his hand.

All heads turned as, finally, the boy Pharaoh slowly stepped out from the pyramid into the

night air. His ceremonial mask glittered as he strode majestically to greet his mighty army.

Kalunga indicated a large rock on the ground. The Pharaoh climbed up on to the platform and surveyed his troops.

On the face of every soldier and beast was a look of dedication and determination. The battle was about to commence and they were ready for anything! The Pharaoh stood there for a few seconds without moving, looking down on the gathered warriors.

Kalunga looked up. He frowned as he noticed a small black and silver object raised up in the boy Pharoah's hand. He didn't remember such an object being buried with his master.

The Pharaoh held the object out towards his troops and then, in one swift movement, he pressed down on something.

No sooner had he done that than a weird high-pitched sound started pouring out of the black and silver box.

Kalunga's fists clenched with rage, but it was too late...

The "Pharaoh" ripped off the ceremonial mask to reveal the face of Max Flash.

When Max had heard Kalunga utter the word "incantation", he'd decided what to do. If Kalunga was going to use a chant to activate the full power of the papyrus, then the only way to reverse this would be to repeat the incantation backwards! And that's where Max's EX4 player had come in so handy – he'd managed to record the whole of the chant.

Playing it backwards to the troops was his way of undoing Kalunga's magic.

As soon as Kalunga realized what was happening, he let out a furious cry. "STOP HIM!"

But at that instant, the reversed chant started to take effect.

One second, this huge army was standing to attention and waiting for their battle command. The next, the soldiers, creatures and their weapons started to shake violently. There were cries of surprise, confusion and fear.

A few seconds more and they were all moving about wildly, like a speeded-up cartoon.

It's working!

Suddenly, their bodies began to deflate. For some, it was their feet that went first; for others, it was their heads. Wherever you looked, soldiers and beasts were popping back into 2-D form.

CHAPTER 21

"NOOOO!" screeched Kalunga. "WE WILL WIN THIS BATTLE!" But even as these words were coming out of his mouth, his face and body were becoming 2-D.

"HELP US!" pleaded Idris, as his hands flattened out. These were followed by his arms and his torso. Sirus followed close behind.

Suddenly, the whole of the 2-D army was drawn back into the pyramid. Max ran to watch as they hurtled through the opening, and were slapped back on to the chamber wall.

Max rushed over to Gazellion's sarcophagus.
The boy Pharaoh was still sitting exactly where
he'd left him. He was concentrating so
intensely on Max's hand-held games console
that he hadn't noticed any of the madness
erupting all around him. But before Max could
reach him, Gazellion himself was suddenly
flattened into 2-D, along with Max's console.

No way! I saved for ages to get that!

As the Pharaoh was pulled up on to the
chamber wall, Max lunged towards Gazellion,
but he was too late. Suddenly a hand grabbed
his arm. He turned round and saw Kalunga.
The Sorcerer was all 2-D apart from his right
hand, with which he now held Max.

Max felt a popping sensation in his toes.
He looked down in horror and saw that they'd
gone 2-D.

Not me as well!

Next his feet went, and then his shins and
knees. The 2-D effect was rapidly spreading

over his body and he was now only centimetres from the wall. Max's thighs popped into 2-D as well and he felt his stomach beginning to flatten out. In a few seconds, he would be on the wall.

The 2-D effect was now travelling down his arms. Soon they were completely flat and his wrists were starting to go. His body crunched against the wall and the 2-D parts of him stuck straight to it. And then he remembered the Laser Stunner.

Quickly!

Max aimed the bracelet at Kalunga and pressed it. Immediately, a white laser shot out catching Kalunga full in the face. He screamed in agony and let go of Max.

Max pressed forward as hard as he could, but his 2-D parts were resistant to being peeled off the walls.

Max tried again, putting all of his energy into one pushing movement. Suddenly, he felt his stomach leave the wall. This was followed by his arms, legs and finally his feet.

He fell to the floor and lay there for a few seconds, breathing hard and trying to process what had just happened. He got up slowly, unsure if the battle was truly over. But the figures on the wall were now completely frozen. They had been reduced to pictures, the life squeezed out of them.

Max stood up and walked closer to the wall, still on his guard just in case Kalunga had any other tricks up his 2-D sleeves. But there was the Sorcerer, his face frozen in a furious expression, his tiny beady eyes looking out from the wall in fury. Wherever Max stood, Kalunga's gaze seemed to follow.

A bit like the Mona Lisa, *only a whole lot uglier!*

And there up on the wall, in Kalunga's left hand, was the *Sorcerer's Venom*.

I think I can safely say it's going to be pretty useless to anyone now!

Max stretched his limbs and checked to see that he had returned to his full 3-D form.

He was all there.

Then he walked up the pathway through the opening, and began the trek back to the site.

I've got quite a story to tell Cullen and Dodd!

CHAPTER 22

The two DFEA agents were astounded by Max's adventure.

"If you hadn't sent that army back to their rightful place on that wall," said Cullen, "then all hell would have broken loose. We would have badly failed our mission and let an ancient Egyptian army march on Cairo."

"Too right," nodded Dodd. "Can you imagine what would have happened? You'd have had a gigantic battle between modern and ancient, with all sorts of magic and sorcery thrown in."

Max suddenly caught sight of Professor Blythe – he'd completely forgotten about him!

Dodd seemed to read his mind. "You're thinking we should tell the Professor, right?"

Max nodded.

"He needs to be shown Gazellion's chamber," said Cullen, "and I have an idea who should act as his guide."

Together they went over to the Professor. He wasn't that happy to see Max, and he was even less happy about the idea of leaving his dig.

"But the Denubi Pyramid has been thoroughly excavated," he said irritably. "There's nothing new to discover there."

"I promise you it will be worth it," Cullen reassured him.

The Professor complained the whole jeep ride to the pyramid.

But as the jeep drove round the perimeter and the large opening came into view, his mouth dropped open. The vehicle drew to a

halt and they jumped out.

The Professor gazed round Gazellion's burial chamber in stunned silence, as Max led him inside. When he finally found his voice, he turned to face Max.

"And YOU discovered all of this?" he exclaimed, his face a mix of awe and delight.

Max nodded.

"But it's odd that Gazellion isn't inside his sarcophagus," muttered the Professor.

"We do have his ceremonial mask," said Max, pointing out the blue and gold face piece.

"What a fine idea it was to have you on my dig. I've always thought children have a big part to play in matters of excavation," said the ecstatic Professor.

"Many more people will believe it's all genuine if you say YOU found it," said Max.

"Now that would be totally unfair and unacceptable," the Professor replied with a stern shake of his head.

"Think of what other archaeologists would say," Max insisted.

The Professor's resolute expression quickly melted. "There is that," he nodded with a faraway look in his eyes. "Maybe it would be a good idea... All in the interests of archaeology, of course."

"Of course!" agreed Max.

But the Professor had noticed something else, and he was striding across the chamber towards the wall on which the image of Gazellion had been imprinted.

Blythe took out a magnifying glass and held

it up to the image of the boy Pharaoh. Max exchanged looks with Cullen and Dodd.

"Remarkable," observed the Professor, calling Max over. "You see that thing the Pharaoh figure is holding."

Max followed his gaze and winced.

"I know this sounds strange," went on Blythe, "but that looks remarkably similar to one of those hand-held games thingies so beloved by the young nowadays."

"Weird, isn't it," agreed Max sheepishly, "but I suppose lots of ancient things look quite like modern things, don't they?"

MAX FLASH MISSION4

CHAPTER 23

Three hours later, Max, Cullen and Dodd were on a flight home. Max's dad was waiting in arrivals at the airport. He gave Max a big hug, and then shook hands with Cullen and Dodd.

"Your son did us proud out there," said Cullen.

"Yes," nodded Dodd. "Without him, utter chaos would have ensued."

Max went over all the details of his mission with his dad on the drive home. When they got back, Mum said she wanted a blow-by-

blow account too, but first he had to see Zavonne, who was waiting for the mission debrief.

When Max got down to the Communications Centre, Zavonne's face was already on the screen.

"I have already spoken to Cullen and Dodd," Zavonne began. "They were full of praise for you."

At last! Zavonne is finally going to say something positive about me!

"However, I think you should have replaced Gazellion's sarcophagus lid before showing the chamber to Professor Blythe," she said.

Max was dumbfounded.

"But it weighed a ton," he protested.

"There are ways and means," Zavonne replied curtly.

Max tried not to feel disappointed, but he couldn't help it. Would the DFEA ice queen ever praise him?

"And you're sure the *Sorcerer's Venom* is safely on the chamber wall?" she enquired.

"A hundred per cent," Max replied. "I don't think it'll be troubling anyone again."

"That is satisfactory," replied Zavonne.

"Er, Zavonne," said Max, "there is something I wanted to ask you."

"Go on," she said.

"In the battle to turn all of the 3-D figures back to 2-D, Gazellion took my hand-held games console with him. It's up there on the wall, too."

Zavonne arched an eyebrow. "What are you getting at?" she asked.

Max swallowed nervously. "I'm asking whether the DFEA could buy me a replacement under their wear and tear guidelines."

Zavonne tutted. "We have no such guidelines," she replied. "If an article gets damaged, the Operative is expected to replace it themselves."

Wow! She's big on perks, isn't she?

"How about paying for half—"

But Max didn't get to finish his sentence, as the image of Zavonne disappeared from the screen.

The cheek of it, thought Max as he wandered upstairs to find his parents and get something decent to eat. *I put myself in grave danger and lose the console for my troubles! That doesn't seem fair!*

EPILOGUE

"Psst," whispered Sirus.

"What is it?" asked Idris.

"Do you reckon there are any 2-D bakers round here who might make 2-D bread?"

Idris sighed. "We're only drawings now, Sirus; we don't need to eat."

"But I'm hungry," Sirus moaned, "and my tummy is complaining."

"Why don't you have a go on that games console Gazellion was using; it'll take your mind off things."

Sirus thought about this.

"Your Highness!" called Idris. "Can Sirus borrow that games thingy?"

"Haven't got it," replied Gazellion.

"I'VE got it," hissed Kalunga, "and I'm nearly on level 5 of Goblin Supremacy. No one gets it until I'm on Level 10."

Sirus sighed wearily.

"How about counting grains of sand on the floor out there in the burial chamber?" suggested Idris.

"We already did that," said Sirus.

"Well, let's try again," suggested Idris. Sirus felt his tummy rumble. "OK," he conceded. "I'll start. 1, 2, 3... "

MAX FLASH
MISSIONS
SUB ZERO

Jonny Zucker

ICE AND SNOW MONSTERS ARE ON THE PROWL!